For Mike and Kathryn Tickell — D. A.

For Carly — L. P.

THE DAM

David Almond

illustrated by
Levi Pinfold

CANDLEWICK STUDIO
an imprint of Candlewick Press

He woke her early.

"Bring your fiddle," he said.

The day was dawning.

Into the valley they walked.

"This will be gone," he told her.

"And this."

"And this will be washed away."

"And this will never be seen again."

"And this will drown."

"And these can never live here again."

The dam was almost done.

"Archie Dagg the piper played here.
And Gracie Gray, she of the gorgeous voice.

"There were dances here.
There were parties.

"I came as a boy to hear them.
I brought you as a little girl. Remember?"

"Yes. Willy Taylor and his lovely violin.
The piccolo of Billy Ballantine."

"Bill Scott taught you the songs in there.
Remember his songbook?"

"I hear them still."

"Take no notice.

There's no danger."

"Come inside now."

"Now play.

Play for all that are gone

and for all that are still to come.

Play, Kathryn, play."

"Sing, Daddy, sing.

Dance, Daddy, dance."

"Now this house. Now this one. Now this one."

They filled the houses with music.

The birds heard.

The beasts heard.

The earth heard.

The trees heard.

The ghosts heard.

The day was darkening.

Out of the valley they walked.

The dam was sealed.

The water rose.

This disappeared.

This was covered over.

This was drowned.

The lake is beautiful.

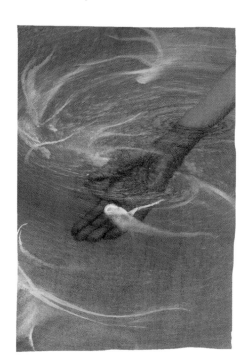

Behind the dam,

within the water, the music stays,

will never be gone.

we hear it when we walk the shores,

as we sail its satin surface,

as we fish its fertile waters,

as we paddle in its shallows,

as we lie beside it in the sun,

as we stare toward the stars.

The music rises.

It continues.

We hear it in the birds

and in the waves

and in the leaves

and in the grass.

We hear it when we are nearby,

when we are far away,

when we remember,

when we dream.

The music is inside us.

It flows through all the dams in us.

It makes us play.

It makes us sing.

It makes us dance.

This is a true story. It was told to me by Mike Tickell and his daughter, Kathryn Tickell. The Kielder Dam was constructed in the wilds of Northumberland, England, in 1981. In the valley behind it, there were farms, homes, a school, a stretch of railway. Many musicians—fiddlers, pipe players, singers—played there, as they did in all the valleys of Northumberland. Once the dam was finished, the valley would be flooded. The buildings were boarded up and the people who lived there were rehoused. Kathryn was a young girl at the time. Just before the dam was

finished, Mike took her into the valley. He tore the boards off the windows and they climbed inside and Kathryn played the last music that would ever be heard there. Then the dam was completed and the water rose, creating what is now Kielder Water, a place that people visit to sail, to fish, to walk, to gaze into the astonishing night skies. Kathryn grew up to become one of the world's great folk musicians and composers. Mike is a singer and songwriter. The musical tradition thrives. Northumberland continues to be beautiful and wild.

First U.S. edition 2018. Library of Congress Catalog Card Number pending. ISBN 978-0-7636-9597-2. This book was typeset in Bookman Old Style. The illustrations were done in charcoal, ink, pastel, and digitally. Candlewick Press, 99 Dover Street, Somerville, Massachusetts 02144. visit us at www.candlewickstudio.com. Printed in Shenzhen, Guangdong, China. 18 19 20 21 22 23 CCP 10 9 8 7 6 5 4 3 2 1